Troublemaker

Troublemaker

LYNN HALL

illustrated by Joseph Cellini

FOLLETT PUBLISHING COMPANY
Chicago

ISBN 0-695-40479-2   Titan binding
ISBN 0-695-80479-0   Trade binding

Library of Congress Catalog Card Number: 74-78455

First Printing

CHAPTER ONE

IT WAS MORNING, nearly six, but the northern Michigan woods were still black on black, giant pine-tree shapes against the paler snow-covered ground. The moon was low; the sun had not yet appeared.

Squares of denser black marked the buildings of Crosleys' Sawmill—the Crosleys' house on one side of the narrow road, a few small buildings on the other. From the smallest of these, suddenly, came a block of light.

The door opened, and a half-grown boy slipped out. Hampered by his unbuckled, man-sized overshoes, he ran around the corner of the shack toward the outhouse. In a moment he came back, still running. He slowed just long enough to pack up a snowball, then slipped back into the shack.

Willis shut the door quietly behind him. He didn't want to wake Mary Lee by any such humane methods as the sound of a door slamming. She was still asleep on the couch with her back toward Willis and her knees curled up against the cushions. Her breath came up in silver puffs, and for every puff there was a wheeze.

As quietly as his jingling boot buckles allowed, Willis moved to the couch, lifted the blanket from his sister's back, and mashed his snowball against her skin.

She yelped and came flailing up out of her sleep.

"I'm going to get you—Willie." The "Willie" was whispered so low it was lost in her wheezing, but it was a small revenge. She scrubbed her back dry with the blanket and glowered up at him.

Willis turned away and lit the two-burner kerosene camp stove that cooked all their meals and heated their wash water.

"Hurry up and get dressed," he said as he dipped water for the coffeepot. "You have to go with me. We're going to get a big old buck deer this morning, and you have to help me drag it home."

"Not me," Mary Lee said. She glanced through the open door to the back room and saw the bed was empty. She raised her voice from whisper to normal. "Dad didn't get back last night?"

Willis shook his head.

"Well," she said flatly, "you can go hunt all you want, but I'm not going to miss any more school. I'm getting too far behind."

She pulled her jeans and flannel shirt up from the floor and took them under the blanket with her.

It was not modesty but cold that made her dress under the blanket.

"You are too going with me, so just shut up about it." Willis cut himself a thick chunk of bread, but he didn't cut her one, nor did he pour a second mug of coffee. She could get her own breakfast. Willis was beginning to feel the hot, senseless fury toward Mary Lee that came, sometimes, and frightened him nearly as much as it frightened her.

He didn't like to be reminded that she liked school and he didn't. It was the high-class people who liked school. Town kids. Kids who got good grades and joined clubs and got elected to things. Not that he'd want to be that kind of person himself, but it infuriated him when Mary Lee leaned in that direction. He had been compelled to find an excuse to beat her up last year when she got to be hall monitor.

He waited with vocal impatience while she ran to the outhouse, then stuffed down her breakfast of bread and coffee. She was dressed entirely in his outgrown clothes. That satisfied him.

"I'm not going hunting with you," she said again as she ate. Her hair stood up in spikes. So did his, but he never thought about his own hair.

"Yes, you are, and hurry up."

"I don't know why you always make me go with you. You don't let me talk, and you won't let me shoot. You don't *really* need me. I'd think you'd rather go by yourself."

Willis threw her jacket at her.

"You're coming, so just shut up about it. And quit sniffing."

"I can't help it. I've got a cold. Where's my mittens? I'll come with you till time for the school bus, and then I'm cutting out."

The eastern sky was shading to pale green as they left the shack, and there were lights in the Crosleys' kitchen window. Willis led the way along a rutted logging track, and then cross-country through a stand of second-growth jack pine. He had a pretty good idea of where he could get a shot at the buck this time of the day, and he headed in that direction.

The old rifle felt good in the crook of his arm, and the cold felt good against his face. The only thing that annoyed him was the sound of Mary Lee, sniffling and wheezing six steps behind him. He wished he hadn't made her come along. His dad could have helped him later with the buck. But she'd put up such a fuss about not wanting to go that he just had to make her go.

After twenty minutes of slogging through the snow they got to where they were heading, a low bluff overlooking a stream bed. Willis took his position where the shrubs hid him from the deer path below and yet gave him a clear shot at anything that passed along the path. He motioned Mary Lee back out of sight.

"I wi—"

"Shhh!" He turned on her and threatened

death with his eyes. "Don't you dare make a sound."

"But I think I'm going to sneeze."

"You sneeze and I'll kill you."

There was a soundless movement below. An old buck deer moved slowly into sight.

Willis raised the rifle.

Mary Lee sucked in her breath.

The buck raised its head.

Mary Lee sneezed. The buck bolted. Willis shot, a fraction of a second too late.

His fury was too vast to be contained in his narrow thirteen-year-old body. It blanked his mind and blocked his vision, leaving him with no sensation but that of rocking darkness. When the moment passed, he found himself looking down the sights of his rifle. Centered in the sights was the face of Mary Lee, skin gray, eyes glazed with terror.

He lowered the gun. "Get the hell out of here," he whispered.

She turned and fled.

When she was safely gone, Willis allowed his muscles to relax into trembling spasms. His stomach rejected its breakfast, and he began to sweat. His legs held up just long enough to get him to a rock and lower him down. He sat, unaware that the snow on the rock was soaking through to his skin. He could feel only the terror of his hands pointing a loaded rifle at his sister's head.

No forgivable boyish roughhousing this time. No excuses of a dead mother and a drunk father.

No mild-voiced Mrs. Crosley saying, "Willis, don't be a troublemaker. You don't want to end up in jail, do you?"

This was a nightmare, and his hands had almost done it. His mind wasn't even working, but his hands had almost shot her.

CHAPTER TWO

H E WAITED UNTIL Mary Lee had time to get back home and catch the school bus. Then he followed. His mind was hardening by that time. He had always known he wasn't any Sunday School kid. He had already pretty much decided he would probably end up a con man or a master thief, either of which might involve some shooting from time to time; so, he reasoned, he might as well get used to the feel of it.

But he still didn't much like the taste it left in his mouth.

The school bus had come and gone by the time he got back to the mill, and the big saw was already screaming into the day's work. Willis could see his father manning the controls of the giant blade. Big Red was unshaved and wearing yesterday's clothes, but he appeared to be sober enough. He was not a particularly large man, and his hair and beard were as much gray as red, but the name stuck. Willis waved at his father, and at Clement, who was feeding the slabbed log into the blade. He put the rifle away in the shack and came back out again.

The blade sang to a stop.

"Get anything?" Red shouted down.

Willis shook his head.

"You missed the bus."

"I know it. I'll walk." He waved at them both, and at Mr. Crosley, who was backing the truck toward him; then he set out down the road toward town.

It was a dangerous place to go, since he didn't intend to go to school and have to explain why he was late, and since he was still on probation from trying to steal rifle cartridges from the hardware store last spring. One of the rules of his probation was no skipping school, so he was definitely taking a chance, hanging around town. But he felt like taking a chance. He felt like walking on a ledge of a high building, or cutting himself open and seeing if somebody would get him to the hospital in time to save him from bleeding to death.

The town was small, about twelve blocks square, and Willis knew every street and alley, railroad track and footpath. Today he took a fugitive route along the railroad track, with occasional shortcuts across backyards and down alleys. He headed in the general direction of the train depot. The cold was beginning to hurt his feet and forehead, and the depot offered warmth, with no questions asked.

Suddenly he stopped walking and pressed back

into a lilac hedge. Just ahead, the dogcatcher's truck was backing toward the high fenced pen behind the dog pound. Willis wasn't sure what connection, if any, there was between dogcatchers, policemen, and truant officers, but the breeds seemed so similar that he distrusted them all, just to be on the safe side.

He stood absolutely motionless while the dog-catcher got out of the truck and walked around toward the back of it. The bare-branched lilac bush offered scant camouflage. The smallest move-ment might give him away. He stopped breathing.

The dogcatcher turned away from Willis and opened the cagelike rear door of the truck. He reached in, pulled out something cat-sized and brown, and shoved it inside the pen, where half a dozen dogs of varied sizes waited. Then he lit a cigarette, examined the torn thumb of his glove, and finally went into the pound office.

Inside the pen a German shepherd bitch ap-proached the new arrival. The brown pup crouched as motionless as Willis in the lilac bush while the shepherd lowered her head toward him. Her lip curled, her tail stiffened, the hair on her withers rose on end. The other dogs drew close around her, watching her.

Suddenly she was a snarling blur and the pup was out of sight under her. The other dogs snarled, barked, yipped, and danced around her, pulling at her in their excitement.

It lasted only a moment. Then the brown pup

was trembling in the far corner of the pen, with blood dripping from a torn ear, and the shepherd bitch was walking off the other way. She had made her point. For the time being, she was satisfied.

Willis stared for a long time at the brown pup. In spite of the inch-thick puppy wool, it was obvious, even from where Willis stood, that the pup was dangerously thin. The animal sat, haunches braced in the corner of the fence, head up, eyes watching the German shepherd. He was no longer trembling. He seemed to have accepted the fact that life was a series of assaults.

He looks about like I feel sometimes, Willis thought.

For the past few years, ever since Willis began to realize that he wasn't much good, he had done a lot of thinking about how it would feel to be locked up in jail. He had imagined himself, eighty skinny pounds of himself, being shoved into a cage full of towering men with knives up their sleeves. There'd be no Mary Lee for him to push around then; instead, *he* would be on the receiving end.

Even if he didn't get hurt, he thought probably the confinement would kill him. Every day of his life that he could remember, he had come and gone as he wanted to. School had irritated him almost unbearably at first, but he had eventually adjusted his life around the fact of school. Even then, all of his nonschool hours were his to fill in whatever way he wanted. Sometimes the thought of the confinement of jail was enough to make him want to stay out of trouble.

The brown pup got up, turned around, and began to dig at the base of the fence. The pen floor was concrete, but the pup dug on with rhythmic fruitlessness.

As Willis watched, he began to feel, in his own fingertips, the scraping cement. He felt the desperation, the terror, the choking need to be free from that pen.

With a glance toward the office window, he crouched and ran across the alley to the fence. He kneeled close to the pup. The pup stopped digging, ducked back a step, then came forward. His tail began to wag; his eyes brightened and met Willis's. He pressed his bony shoulder against the two fingers Willis stuck through the fence.

At the warm furry touch some deep tightness in Willis was shaken loose. This dog was his.

This dog was him.

Willis left the alley and began to lope the five blocks to school. His dislike of the place was forgotten now, in his need to talk to Mary Lee and to George Schmidt. Besides, he was suddenly violently hungry.

He got to the old brick building just in time to duck into the hot lunch line in the cafeteria. Luck was on his side. George was just three people up the line from him.

"Hey, Schmidt."

George turned around. "Hi.· Where were you this morning?"

"Had to help my dad, and I missed the bus. I had to walk all the way in." Willis knew, and George knew, that he had not walked two miles for the love of school, but it was fun to pretend anyway. "Hey, listen. You got your dog from the pound last year, didn't you?"

"Yeah. Why?"

"Keep moving, boys." The teacher who was at the little table, punching hot lunch cards, frowned at them, but it was a token, impersonal frown.

"Did you have to pay for it, or do they just give the dogs away?"

"No, we had to pay. I think it was two dollars for the dog and another three for the license or some kind of shot or something. But I remember it was five dollars all together, because that was my birthday money from my aunt. Why?"

"Oh, I just wondered. What is it today, macaroni and cheese?"

He didn't want to tell George about the brown pup. The way his luck had been running lately, George would probably know who the puppy belonged to, or something. Mary Lee was the only one he could trust, and he wouldn't be able to talk to her till after lunch, because she was sitting where she always sat, with a table full of girls, and he must sit with George and the rest of the sixth-grade boys.

There were often times, such as now, when he would have preferred Mary Lee's company to theirs, but he would no more approach the girls' table than she would approach his.

He caught up with her in the hall, after he'd scraped his plate bare of macaroni and cheese. Her face was tight and guarded, but Willis had forgotten for the moment that he had almost shot her.

"You have to stay in town with me after school," he said, talking down his shirt front so nobody would overhear. "We got a very important mission, and we can't do it till after it gets dark."

The tightness left her face. "What are we going to do?" She kindled to his enthusiasm.

"We're going to get a friend of mine out of jail," he whispered.

By five-thirty the town was dark, and so were the windows of the dog pound. For the last half hour Willis and Mary Lee had been drifting around the end of the alley, taking turns throwing snowballs at the light pole, taking running slides on the icy sidewalk, glancing from time to time toward the rear of the dog pound, three backyards away. But now the pound was deserted.

"Come on," Willis whispered.

They moved up the alley, avoiding bars of light from kitchen windows, staying close to hedges and garages. When they reached the pen, Willis stopped.

"Ah, curse it," he said. "The dogs are inside."

It hadn't occurred to him that the job would be any more complicated than just climbing the fence and scooping up his dog.

"What are you going to do now, break in?" Mary Lee was close beside him, shivering.

He didn't bother to answer. Instead, he went to the window at the side of the building and tried it. It opened.

He nodded toward the ground. "Get down on your hands and knees. I need a step up."

"I don't think you better go in there, Willis. You could get thrown in jail or reform school or something. Why don't you just try to get the five dollars from somewhere if you want him that bad?"

He sighed, impatiently. "Because, stupid, like I told you before, the big dogs will kill him if I don't get him out of there. They almost did already. If you're too scared to help, you can just go on home. I'll do it myself."

Slowly Mary Lee got down on all fours under the window. Snow fell into the tops of her mittens.

"Ouch. Watch where you step," she snapped.

He shifted his foot from the middle of her back to the steadier support of her hips, and vaulted up to where he could squirm through the window.

From the dark area to his left came a sudden volley of barking, but as soon as he spoke to the dogs, they fell quiet, listening. His eyes adjusted to the darkness, at least enough to make out the shapes of desk, file cabinets, and a bank of cages along the back wall. The dogs shifted, wagged, shuffled their newspaper bedding, but they didn't bark again.

As Willis moved toward the cages, he heard a high, soft whimpering, a sound of uncontrollable anticipation. It came from the lowest of all the sets of reflecting eyes that watched him.

"Hang on there, buster. I'm going to get you out of there right now."

He felt as though he were moving in a slow-motion dream, but it was actually little more than a minute before the pup was handed out the window to Mary Lee, and Willis scraped through the opening and dropped down beside her. He closed the window, mussed up their snowy tracks, and then, slowly, relishing the moment, he took the puppy in his hands.

"I got him. I really got him," he said softly.

"Let's get out of here," Mary Lee said.

With the puppy zipped inside Willis's jacket, they set out down the alley, beside the tracks, and finally along the shoulder of the road home.

CHAPTER THREE

IT WAS A SATURDAY MORNING late in May. By the time Mary Lee began jerking and stirring and coming up out of her nest on the couch, Willis had already caught and cleaned three small trout. It was the smell of their frying on the camp stove that finally woke her.

As soon as she moved, the half-grown brown dog wagged himself across the floor and tried to lick her face.

"Buster. Leave her be," Willis said over his shoulder while he turned the fish. The dog came bouncing back to him.

Mary Lee rubbed her nose, hard, against her palm and sat up. It always took her several minutes to come to life. Willis woke with every sense alert, and he had little patience with her morning fuzziness.

"We been up for two hours already, haven't

we, Buster? I got fish for breakfast, so hurry up. We're not waiting for you."

Mary Lee muttered, "Cantaloupe for breakfast, honey and a bun. Put your shoes and stockings on and run, run, run."

Willis pulled three plates from the pile of unwashed dishes on the table that held the washbasin. The plates had only the residue of last night's meatloaf—leftovers from Mrs. Crosley—nothing that needed washing off, as far as Willis was concerned. He put two of the fish on plates. The third fish he broke up between his fingers and, with clinical thoroughness, removed every tiny bone. Then he set the plate of crumbled fish on the floor.

"Wait!" he commanded.

Buster froze in position, eyes fastened on the plate, muscles knotted.

"Okay," Willis said. The plate was empty before the release word had died from the air. Only then did Willis sit down to his own plate. The pup came and leaned against the boy's leg. He had doubled in size in the past two months and had fattened considerably. Willis called him a collie; he was probably as close to that general type as to any other.

The meal was a silent one. It would probably be their only meal of the day, and they were both intent on the food. Neither of them mentioned what was in their minds—that this was the fifth day, that it looked as though it might be another three-monther.

Willis scraped up the last of his fish and sat twirling one of Buster's ears with an index finger. He could remember half a dozen times like this, when Red had simply disappeared. There was never any warning, just a letter after he'd been gone a while, saying he was out west, or down south, or up in Canada, looking for a better job, a better place for them. But always before, there had been at least one or two of the older kids at home, to take over. Six half-brothers and half-sisters, from previous marriages. The shack had been unbearably crowded until they had begun, one by one, to leave.

Now, for the first time, Willis wished it weren't just he and Mary Lee left at home. Three months was an awfully long time for Mr. Crosley to hold off hiring somebody else for Red's job. A long time to live on fish when he could catch them, squirrels when he could shoot them, Mary Lee's dwindling rabbit stock. And Mrs. Crosley's leftovers.

A rusty pickup truck coated with dust coasted to a stop outside the shack.

"Oh, good. Kershaws," Mary Lee said. "Rabbit customers." She unwound her feet from the chair rung and ran outside.

Willis watched from the window. He didn't trust Mary Lee any more. Twice he had caught her trying to tell him she'd sold only one rabbit when she had actually sold two. The first time, he had only twisted her arm up hard behind her back and threatened her. The second time, his rage was uncontrollable. He had hurt her then. He was sick afterwards, and had tried not to think of it again, but he often dreamed about it, and about the day he had almost shot her. He always woke, terrified, from those dreams.

Mary Lee came into sight carrying a rusted cage with two rabbits in it. Mr. Kershaw counted the money into her hand, rumpled her hair, and drove away. Without looking toward Willis's window, she came back into the shack.

"Two of them," she said, holding out the hand with the money in it.

"I know it. I was watching you." He took his half, a dollar-fifty.

"I don't know why you should get half, anyway," she muttered. "They're my rabbits."

"I get half because I'm your older brother—"

"Year and a half," she muttered.

"—and because I'll beat the living daylights out of you if you don't give it to me."

She started moving around the room, folding her blanket, picking up Buster's dish. "Well, one of these days you'll take off, like the older kids, and then I won't have to give you anything."

"Listen, when I take off, you're coming, too. You're going to be my accomplice when I'm a mastermind con artist."

She shook her head. "I'm going to stay right here and be a rabbit raiser. And you're not going to be a con artist, either. You'll grow up and go in the army or go to work in a sawmill someplace, like everybody else, so you might as well quit talking like that."

"Huh. You don't know anything. Come on, Buster. At least I got one friend."

He went outside. Around him, in a loose crescent, were the buildings of the mill—small sheds and ramps, the long open-sided structure that housed the mammoth saw. There was a second shack, larger than Red's but no more comfortable, where Clement and his wife and small children had lived until last year. Then they had rented a farmhouse two miles away. Clement said it was because they'd paid off their debts and could afford a better place. Other people said it was because of some trouble between Red and Clement's wife. Probably both, Willis had thought at the time.

He saw Clement, now, loading the small truck from the stack where the shiplap was drying. Following an impulse that was connected with his fear of what would happen to him, and to Buster, if Red got fired, Willis went down to the truck and began to help load. He stood in the truck bed and pulled the boards up as Clement fed them to him.

Clement looked the way Willis imagined Paul Bunyan would look—large, hard, dark, and square-faced, with heavy brows and a constantly sprouting beard.

"Heard anything from your dad yet?" Clement asked.

"Nope."

"Didn't say anything about where he might be going, before he took off?"

"Nope. He never does. He just disappears, but he always comes back. About three months generally."

"Ninety days," Clement said softly.

"What do you mean, ninety days?"

"Oh, ninety days could mean a lot of things. Could mean—summer vacation. Could mean— ninety days in the tank for habitual drunk driving. Could mean a lot of things."

Almost as a reflex action, Willis began to get angry, but the anger faded. Clement had said nothing that Willis hadn't already thought. Red's disappearances were too uniform in length to be coincidences, spur-of-the-moment trips in search of a better job. As long as the suspicion had remained unspoken, Willis hadn't given it much thought. Life without Red was a great deal like life with Red, except for the uncertainty of continued food and shelter. But now, having heard someone hint at knowing more than he did, Willis began to want to know for certain.

"This load going to Whitewater, Clement?" he asked in an offhand tone.

"Yep. Just as soon as she's loaded."

Willis nodded, thought a moment, then said, "I think I'll ride along."

CHAPTER FOUR

IT WAS A TWENTY-MILE DRIVE to the county-seat town of Whitewater, over flat, narrow blacktop roads, through jack-pine forests floored with sand. The seat and floor of the truck were piled with tools, rope, a red-and-black wool jacket, two battered Thermos bottles, and a length of chain with links as big as Willis's fist. Willis arranged himself around the junk and held Buster on his lap. The dog's head moved quickly, ceaselessly, from side to side as his eyes followed the backward-spinning scenery beyond the window.

"Where do you want off?" Clement asked when they got to the edge of town.

"By the bridge somewhere. I want to go downtown and walk around a while. I'll meet you back out at the lumberyard when I get through."

Clement looked at the boy. For an instant his square Paul Bunyan face lost its automatic joviality. Concern showed itself. "What are you going to do?"

27

"Nothing. Just mess around. I'll see you."

The main street of Whitewater was built along a small but fast-moving river. In fact, the backs of the store buildings on that side of the street dropped straight down into the water.

Willis got down from the truck at the town's main intersection, and walked across an arched stone bridge toward the courthouse, in its square of park, on the far bank of the river. He carried Buster across his chest, lamb-fashion, partly in fear of the traffic, partly from comfortable habit. He carried the pup whenever he could. At home, whenever he sat down, Buster was immediately in the chair with him, and at night they slept under the blankets together, Buster's head pillowed on Willis's arm, his backbone against the boy's chest.

It was a long climb up the cement steps from street level to the courthouse park, but Willis wasn't tempted to put Buster down. Now, suddenly, he was hanging onto the dog for support.

"It doesn't make any difference whether he's in there or not." Willis spoke silently, but the words were directed to Buster.

Trying to look as though he was just shortcutting across the grass, Willis moved toward the barred basement windows at one corner of the courthouse. The jail was down there. He and some other boys had peered through those windows once, a few years ago, intending to yell something funny down to whoever might be locked inside. But there had been no one in the cells then.

Looking casually in all directions, Willis moved to the nearest window and dropped to his knees. He set Buster down, but kept a restraining hand on the dog's neck.

A few feet inside the window was the cell wall, made not of round bars but of a lattice of iron strips, bolted together every few inches. It kept the prisoners at a safe distance from windows, radiators, and aged brick walls soft enough to be chipped through.

Willis could see only small squares of color through the iron lattice, but it was enough. The blue-and-green plaid flannel was Big Red's back. Through the open window Willis could hear, "Are you going to draw or not?"

And Red's voice answering, "Lookie here. Gin. That's five in a row for me. Man, that was a beautiful hand you dealt me that time. Hope I don't do the same for you." Then staccato sounds of cards being shuffled by a practiced hand.

Willis scooped up the pup and headed back downtown.

"So Dad's in jail," he said silently to Buster as he jounced down the cement steps to the sidewalk. "So what's new? And who cares? He's having a good time in there, doesn't have to work, probably gets better food than he does at home. If he doesn't care, why should we?"

The dog hung limp and warm and heavy in his arms, his head riding across Willis's shoulder.

Two women came toward them on the sidewalk part of the bridge. As they passed Willis, they looked down, curiously, into his face. They stopped talking until he was past, then began again.

"I can't help it if my dad's in jail," he shouted after them furiously but silently. "Oh no, that's silly. They don't know who I am."

Suddenly he wished he had made Mary Lee come along. It hadn't seemed important earlier, because he had Buster to be on his side, but now he needed Mary Lee. He needed her to make him be tough.

He made his usual rounds, but he made them in record speed—dime store, drugstore magazine rack, hardware store hunting and fishing gear department, the Gambles store, the posters in front of the movie theater. Then, after a brief sit on the steps that led up to the dentist's office, just long enough to rest his arms, he started down the main-street highway toward the lumberyard.

A few blocks out, between the DX station and the Farmers Co-op, was the Hires root-beer stand. Suddenly Willis realized he was hungry. He put Buster down long enough to get a foot-long hot dog, French fries, and a large root beer. Half of his rabbit profits for the day.

"Come on, Buster. Over here in the shade."

They went to the far end of the parking lot and sat on the railroad tie that marked the end of the property. Spruce trees from the adjoining backyard shaded them, and the nearest cars full of lunching people were a comfortable distance away.

"Ah, this is living," said Willis, opening the little

sack of food and sucking in its scent. He picked up an empty malt cup and poured into it exactly half of his root beer. The foot-long and the fries were divided into exact halves, too, and put down on a square of waxed paper. Buster watched intently, but made no move toward the food.

"Okay!"

The dog lunged, and the food was gone.

Willis's half of the eating didn't take much longer. "We better get on out to the lumberyard," he said through the last bite. "Don't want old Clement to go off home without us." He picked up Buster and started across the parking lot.

"What'sa matter with your dog?"

The voice came from the car he was passing. There were three teen-aged boys in the car.

"Nothing's the matter with him, stupid," Willis retorted.

"Is he crippled, or just too dumb to walk?" the driver asked, grinning.

"He can walk fine. I'd just rather carry him."

The boys laughed. "I'd just rather carry him," one of them mimicked. "Is that your doll baby, little boy?"

The familiar fury began to come up behind Willis's eyes. He lowered Buster to the ground.

"Come out here and say that, if you've got the guts." His voice shook, but not with fear.

The driver started to open the car door, then hesitated. "Nah, I don't go around hurting little kids. I ain't—"

Willis launched himself at the door, jerked it open, spilling food from the tray, and dragged the man-sized boy out onto the gravel. He was not conscious of what he was doing, only of blurred motion, hammering blows, jarring thrusts, an insult to Buster. He was on his back on the ground, kicking, punching; he was braced against the car; he was bouncing off of the canopy post. He heard nothing but his own ringing brain.

For an instant his vision cleared and he saw Buster swinging in an arc, his mouth clamped around the enemy's leg. He heard a voice saying, "Somebody call the cops!"

He dodged the hands that reached for his throat. With a running tackle he scooped up his dog, then flew across the parking lot and down the road. He didn't stop running till he got to the lumberyard.

The Crosleys' Sawmill truck was empty and waiting. He waved at Clement, who was inside the office, then boosted himself and Buster up into the back of the truck. Finally, sprawled on the truck bed, he breathed out a long, long breath.

When the truck was out of town and rolling along the familiar blacktop, Willis opened his eyes and looked down into the waiting gaze of the dog curled up against his hip. His hand pulled gently on Buster's ear. He grinned.

"We beat the pee-wadding out of that creep, didn't we, old buddy?"

Suddenly he felt great.

CHAPTER FIVE

IT WAS THE LAST DAY OF SCHOOL, just an assembly in the gym and last-minute turning in of books and cleaning out of lockers. Willis felt like doing handsprings over the stair railings or telling off some teachers, but he contented himself with just banging his locker door as loudly as he could. With wild whoops he raced across the grass to the school bus. He got his favorite seat, the single one beside the wheel hump, and settled back with a sigh of pure joy.

No more elementary building! On, on to junior high. At long, long last. With a wave of remembered sickness he thought how it had been this time last year, finding out that he had flunked. The prospect of going through sixth grade again, in the same class as Mary Lee, who was a year and a half younger than he, was very nearly unbearable. But that nightmare was over now. He was moving ahead again, making progress toward that distant dreamed-of day when he would be through with school forever.

Now. Ah, now, he thought. Three months of spending every minute of his time with Buster.

He sat up, eager for his first glimpse of the dog even though the mill road turnoff was still half a mile away.

Oh, no, he reminded himself, he won't be meeting the bus today. It's coming four hours earlier than he's used to. I'll just surprise him when I get home.

The increasingly loud horseplay in the bus went past his head unnoticed. As usual when he was with groups of kids his age, he was sealed off from them. He belonged to himself. He was his own best and only friend, except for Buster, and sometimes Mary Lee. Other boys his age didn't much like him, and he didn't much like them.

A familiar swaying, slowing, of the bus brought him to his feet. Ahead of him, where the girls sat, Mary Lee rose, too, and joined him at the handrail at the front of the bus. They rounded the final small bend and coasted to a stop at the mouth of the mill road. There, in his accustomed place, sat Buster.

The door hissed open; Willis and Mary Lee jumped the steps and landed, running, on the sandy ground.

"Hey, Buster!" Willis dropped his gym clothes to meet the pup's charge. Dog and boy collided in a rough embrace that took them rolling down into the roadside ditch. It was their usual greeting after a day's separation.

When they had sorted themselves out and started the half-mile walk home, Mary Lee said, "How did he know when the bus would be coming?"

"He knows everything, that's how."

"No, really. How did he know, Willis?"

He gave her a long slow look, one eye squinted. "I'll tell you how. He's got ESP, see. He and I can send each other messages with our minds—just our two brains sending out these waves. Like radios. As soon as we got on the bus, I sent him a message that I was coming home."

"Oh, come on."

He ran ahead of her, racing Buster, but he was pondering the same question himself. It hadn't surprised him when Buster had begun meeting the bus at three-thirty, a few weeks ago. That was just habit, he knew. It had to do with the instincts dogs had about telling time. Every morning the pup accompanied him and Mary Lee to the bus stop, and every afternoon at the same time the two of them came home. It was natural enough that Buster would start waiting at the bus stop at three-thirty. But why, today, at eleven-thirty?

He slowed down, and Mary Lee caught up with him. "Do you suppose he sits down there all day, after we get on the bus in the morning?" she asked.

He shrugged and pitched a pinecone at a tree trunk.

36

Crosleys' house came into view through the trees. It was huge compared to the shack, with brown shingles and mustard-colored trim, and a porch that went around three sides of it. To Willis it represented something alien, something he refused to let himself want. But Mary Lee was fascinated by both the house and Mrs. Crosley.

The woman was in the backyard hanging up a load of washing.

"Let's go ask her," Mary Lee said suddenly.

Mrs. Crosley was small, round-faced but thin everywhere else, with black-and-white-streaked hair and tired lines in her face. Her eyes slipped past Willis, but they warmed on Mary Lee.

"Well, did you pass?" she asked.

"Yup, we both did." Mary Lee bounced up as close to the woman as she dared. A few years ago she would have run into a hug, but now she just danced from foot to foot and took Mrs. Crosley's mother-warmth from a distance.

"Here. Give a hand." Mrs. Crosley pulled a bedspread up from the clothes basket and gave Mary Lee a corner. Between them they stretched it out, flapped it, and arranged it over the line.

Since Mary Lee seemed to have forgotten why they'd stopped, Willis said, "Did you happen to notice when Buster went down to meet the bus?"

"Today, you mean?" Mrs. Crosley squinted at him and put two clothespins into her mouth.

"Yeah. We were just wondering how he knew

what time we were coming home, and Mary Lee thought maybe he always waits for me all day, down there."

"No, he doesn't do that, I know, because I see him over by your place during the day. No, let's see. Today he went by about eleven, because I was watching for the mail."

"Hmm." Willis frowned in concentration.

"Wait till I get through here, and I'll show you kids something," Mrs. Crosley said.

She finished hanging the basketful of clothes and led them to the back porch. Mary Lee went inside eagerly, but Willis hung back, disliking the bigness and the quality of the house.

"Come along, Willis." Mrs. Crosley held the screen door open till he was up the stairs and inside. In the kitchen Willis gritted himself against the overpowering shine of the pine paneling, the stove and refrigerator and deep freezer. They were an insult to his shack, which was about the same size as this kitchen and had only the camp stove, the dishpan, the orange-crate cupboard, and the pump outside the door. And he hated the fact that Buster was left outside, pressing his nose against the screen, searching with his eyes for Willis.

Suddenly Buster barked. Across the kitchen floor came a small white puppy who had been asleep in a cardboard box in the pantry. She was of a general spaniel type but with a terrier face. On close inspection she showed pale yellow markings on her ears and back. Beneath her eyes were long rust-colored tearstains.

"Oh, a puppy," Mary Lee said softly. She sat cross-legged on the kitchen floor and received the pup into her lap. "Where did you get it?"

Mrs. Crosley sighed and pulled out a chair for herself. She ignored Willis.

"My sister-in-law brought it out this morning. She'd got it for her kids, but her husband didn't want a dog around the house. So she brought it out here. It's a her."

"Oh, she's cute. Look at her kiss me. She likes me, doesn't she, Willis? Just like Buster and you. What's her name?"

Mrs. Crosley sniffed a long, dry sniff. "They called her Peaches. If you'd like to have her, Mary Lee, you're welcome to her. With our new carpeting in the living room, I don't much want a puppy around."

Mary Lee looked from Mrs. Crosley to Willis with shining eyes.

Willis scowled. In a way it would be okay, he mused, for Mary Lee to have her own dog. Then she wouldn't be trying to make up to Buster all the time. But on the other hand, he hated to let go of the prestige of being the owner of the one dog in the family. And it was hard enough feeding one dog, let alone two.

"I don't know," he said. "I don't know what we'd feed another dog, especially with Dad away and . . ."

He hadn't meant to say that. He and Mary Lee knew where Red was, Mrs. Crosley knew where he was, everybody around there knew, but it was never talked about in front of Willis and Mary Lee. And he certainly didn't want to get into the subject with Mrs. Crosley.

She pushed up from her chair and went into the pantry. "You can take this." She came backing out, dragging a fifty-pound sack of dog food. "My sister-in-law bought it when she got Peaches, and then she didn't have any use for it, so she gave it to me. That ought to last you till your dad gets back to work. I don't think he'll be gone much longer."

Awkwardly they made their way home. Willis struggled with the slippery bulk of the dog food sack, Mary Lee carried the puppy and tried to keep her away from Buster, and Buster circled them both in a frenzy of curiosity.

It would be worth having another dog around, Willis decided, if it meant Buster got half of a fifty-pound sack of real dog food.

CHAPTER SIX

On AN AFTERNOON nearly a month later, Willis stood watching a massive plank going through the saw blade and coming out as two-by-fours. He was bare to the waist, and a fine powdering of sawdust stuck to his sweaty body. The roof of the open-sided saw shed kept the sun off of the workers, but the heat from the saw's motor more than made up for it.

Buster lay watching from the shade of the drying stack, and Mary Lee and Peaches were sitting on top of the mountain of sawdust behind the shed, with their backs to Willis. As the two-by-fours fell free of the blade, Willis wrapped his arms around them and dragged them to the drying stack. Splinters punctured his skin, but they didn't bother him. He'd gotten so many splinters this summer he figured he was more than half jack pine by now, and besides, he enjoyed fishing the splinters out of his skin with a needle, while Mary Lee grimaced and repeated, "Ooo, how can you do that?" In a way that he didn't understand, he reveled in the pain. Somehow he was fascinated by the sight of his own blood.

"Well, would you look who's coming," Clement shouted over the noise of the saw.

Willis looked up. Shortcutting through the trees was his father. With a yelp Mary Lee slid down the sawdust mountain and ran toward Red. She didn't hug him, but she danced in a close circle around him as he came toward the saw shed. Buster rose, barked, came to stand beside Willis.

Mr. Crosley threw the switch that sent the blade singing into silence; then he went forward with Clement to meet Red. Willis stayed where he was. He kept one hand on Buster's head. The other hand, of its own accord, started sweeping wood chips into a pile. He couldn't hear what the men were saying, but he saw Mr. Crosley make a vague friendly gesture, a hand resting briefly on Red's shoulder. Then the group moved into the shade of the shed roof.

"Willis," Red said, nodding.

"Hi, Dad."

"You kids been okay while I was gone?"

"Sure."

Red looked older than Willis remembered him. It had been only two months, but there was a difference. The man looked away from Willis.

"I been up north, looking at the possibilities up there. I should have wrote you kids—"

"Up north at the county jail, you mean." Willis spoke mildly. His father was no longer an important part of his life. For the past two months he and Mary Lee had gotten along just fine, living on the little bit Mr. Crosley paid him for doing the lighter jobs around the mill a few hours a day, and on the fish and squirrels he caught, and on Mary Lee's occasional rabbit sales. Red was okay to have around. He was a nice enough guy when he was sober. But he wasn't important to Willis's survival.

As Red's expression went from blank to embarrassed confusion, Willis began to take pleasure in his power over the man. He went on in a conversational tone.

"What was it this time, drunk and disorderly? Drunk driving? We figured you'd be gone your usual ninety days. Didn't look for you till next month some time. What happened—time off for good behavior?"

Red moved closer to Willis, away from Mary Lee. His voice dropped. "It was drunk driving. The rest I'll explain later. Listen, does your sister . . ." He motioned with his head toward Mary Lee and raised his eyebrows.

"Oh, sure, she knows all about it. Me and her just sit around all the time, talking about our jailbird father. She was going to bake you a cake with a file in it, but we didn't have enough flour."

Suddenly Willis was furious. He wanted to hurt his father any way he could, for standing there like a big bum, trying to lie to them. For being worried about whether Mary Lee knew. Mary Lee! Everyone always worried about Mary Lee.

Before his fury reached the out-of-control point, Willis became aware of Buster standing up against him, front paws on Willis's shoulders. The dog was staring into Willis's eyes with a fixed, bright stare.

Red said, "Your dog's getting right big. He's a good-looking animal, Willie. You're going to have yourself a brag dog there." It was an obvious effort to ingratiate himself, and Willis hardened himself against it.

"Hey, Daddy, look at *my* dog." Mary Lee began shouting and dancing. With tangible relief Red turned to her.

Red and Mary Lee went into the shack, Mr. Crosley turned the saw on again, and Willis went back to catching and dragging two-by-fours. Buster stayed close beside him, pacing back and forth from saw to drying stack as though he were protecting Willis.

The summer passed with the swiftness of all summers. Red's return freed Willis from mill work, and the presence of Buster freed him from having to keep Mary Lee with him whenever he needed company. It became the best summer he could remember. He seldom came home from fishing without at least a small string of triumphs; his aim with the rifle improved to the point where, when he took aim at a squirrel, he was pretty sure of a kill.

And there was Buster. With every day that passed, the dog obsessed Willis more completely.

Rarely were they more than four feet apart, and when they were, invisible forces drew them together again. Willis began sleeping on a cushion of blankets on the shack floor, partly to avoid sharing his father's bed, but mostly to be close to Buster. The dog had no set feeding time, but half of everything that was put before Willis was fed to Buster. And every rat and mole the dog killed was brought as an offering to Willis. The absolute love that shone in the dog's eyes burned into the deepest part of Willis.

On a Saturday afternoon in late summer Willis sat watching Mary Lee and Mrs. Crosley hoe potato hills. He sat on the concrete square that held the old pump. With a lazy bump-bump rhythm he hit the pump handle with his head, feeling the sun-hot metal through his hair. If he'd sat a few feet to the left, he'd have been in the shade, but he enjoyed the sense of being burned, and surviving.

Buster was in the shady grass nearby, lying in his U-position, on his back with his four legs flopped and folded, his head twisted around for balance. He was asleep but still tuned to Willis.

Peaches was tied on the back porch to keep her from bouncing through the garden and breaking stalks.

Willis watched Mary Lee and Mrs. Crosley as they chopped their way slowly down the length of the garden. He wondered why he wasn't somewhere else, doing something. But still he sat idly bumping the pump handle. Their voices came to him, but he wasn't working at listening to them.

"You take that next row, dear. Then we won't be in each other's way. There's my good little helper."

Oh, ick, Willis thought. "There's my good little helper." You stupid old bat. Don't you know Mary Lee only helps you because you give her tomatoes?

He knew that wasn't strictly true, but it rankled in Willis, the way Mrs. Crosley always called Mary Lee "dear." It was sickening.

After a while Mary Lee came and stood in front of him. Peaches darted around her feet, and in her arms she cradled eight dark red tomatoes.

"I'm going home. Are you coming?"

He didn't feel like moving, but he darn well wasn't going to sit in Mrs. Crosley's backyard alone. He whistled Buster up out of his sleep and helped himself to the biggest tomato. It was warm from the sun. He exploded it with his teeth and sucked in its acid juice.

"What about the dog show?" Mary Lee asked. "Should we go?"

"What dog show?"

"Weren't you listening? Mrs. Crosley was just talking about it. I figured you heard. She saw a poster in the grocery store this morning. It's a dog show, in Whitewater, all day tomorrow at the fairgrounds. Should we go?"

Willis turned away from the eagerness in her voice. He had never been to a dog show, and it kin-

dled his interest. He knew, immediately, that he and Buster were going to the show. But not Mary Lee. He didn't want her along. Mrs. Crosley's dear little Mary Lee needed to be shoved back down to her proper level.

CHAPTER SEVEN

HE LEFT THE HOUSE before the sun was up, before Mary Lee was up. The road to Whitewater was bare of traffic that early on a Sunday morning, and it took half of the morning to walk and hitchhike the twenty miles to town. Most of the drivers who started to slow down when they saw Willis speeded up again when they saw the dog beside him. But eventually he was invited into the back of an old pickup truck, which took him all the way to the entrance of the fairgrounds.

Willis waved his thanks to the driver and turned to the problem before him: getting into the show. A line of cars was moving slowly through the fairgrounds gate, past a man who was obviously taking admissions. Willis started down the road, away from the gate.

"Don't worry, Buster. This won't be hard at all."

At the corner of the huge fairgrounds property they left the road and moved through the long grass of someone's pasture, following the high fairgrounds fence. Buster looked with keen interest at the cattle who watched them, but he stayed close to Willis.

49

Behind the 4-H Sheep Barn the high fence gave way to low woven wire fencing that sagged between the posts in a clear invitation. Willis and Buster were over the fence and moving toward the center of activity so smoothly they hardly had time to think how smart they were.

Beyond the sheep barns the grounds were alive with moving figures. Acres of cars, campers, and vans shimmered in the sun. Everywhere Willis looked there were dogs being groomed on chrome tables, dogs being led or carried in all directions. Through the mass of people and dogs Willis could see a double row of square paddocks, blocked off from the crowds by low white fences. These seemed to be the center of the excitement.

Off to one side, away from the density of the crowds, were two larger enclosures. A smaller group of people sat around the fences, on the ground or in lawn chairs. Willis eased around the edges of the clusters of spectators until he was beside the farthest of the two remote rings. He had a sudden strong feeling that Buster shouldn't be here, with all these ritzy dogs, and of course if Buster didn't belong, then neither did he. But having made the long trip, he was determined to stay till someone threw him out.

He went to the far side of the ring, where only a few watchers were sitting. Trying to make himself as small as possible, he sat on the ground and pulled Buster down across his lap. Immediately he was absorbed by what was going on in the ring, just a few feet in front of him.

The ring held only one dog, a few people, and

two white wooden jumps. The dog sat tensely beside a man who appeared to be his owner. Willis stared at the dog. It was a poodle, densely black and as big as Buster, with a huge lionlike mane around his neck. He was magnificent.

"Is that really a poodle?" he asked of the woman who sat a few feet away. For the moment he forgot he was in hiding.

The woman was hefty, middle-aged, and leathery. She sat in a lawn chair that had an umbrella attached to one arm, so her face was in the shade, indistinct to Willis's sun-smarting eyes.

"Standard poodle," she said shortly. She glanced down at Buster, but said nothing about him.

"Oh. I never saw one that big before."

There was a pause; then the woman said, "He's good. Watch him. That's the judge coming out, now."

A woman in a white pants suit walked to the center of the ring. She wrote something on the clipboard she carried, then spoke to the man with the poodle. "Are you ready?"

"Yes, ma'am," came the answer.

"You may begin."

The woman's lawn chair creaked as she leaned toward Willis. "If he gets a passing score today, he'll have his C.D.X."

Willis looked puzzled.

"That's an obedience degree. He's already got his C.D. Now he's going for the next degree, you understand?"

"Oh, uh-huh." Willis nodded.

The dog, at his owner's command, was retrieving tossed wooden dumbbells, first in the open space between the jumps, and then over the high jump. When he sailed over the four-foot jump with the power and grace of a Thoroughbred, huge mane flying, dumbbell held proudly in his mouth, Willis stared with shining eyes. He was seeing Buster leaping obstacles on command.

"Is it very hard to teach them to do that?" he asked.

"Depends on the dog," the woman said crisply. "Some are smart, and some are dumb. Most dogs can learn, though, if you take the time and work with them."

"My dog's smart. He's probably about the smartest dog around here."

The woman looked down again at Buster. "I bet he is." There was a smile in her voice. " 'Course you realize you couldn't show him. Not in a regular dog show."

Willis flared. "Why not, if he can do the tricks?"

"Not tricks. Commands. You can't show a dog that isn't a purebred."

Willis's arms tightened around Buster's neck. "That's not any fair. Buster's better than any old fancy dog!"

"Rules," she said simply.

Willis snorted, then got to his feet. "Come on, Buster. Let's get out of here. Stuck-up people anyhow."

He left in a steaming rage, not even waiting to be thrown out.

CHAPTER EIGHT

WILLIS SIMMERED for two weeks, bending
back and forth between contempt for the dog show
world that had insulted Buster, and memories of the
black poodle sailing over the jumps. It became a
thing he had to prove, that Buster was as smart as
any of them.

One day he went into town and mentally pushed
himself up the steps of the public library. He felt
sharply uncomfortable in there, but he made himself
go through with it, and ten minutes later he escaped,
victorious.

"I got it," he shouted to the waiting dog.

In his hand was a book titled *Training You To
Train Your Dog*.

"You know what? I really am going to make a
brag dog out of you, like Dad said. You might not
be a show dog or a C.D.X. or whatever that woman
said, but I'll bet you're going to be the best-trained
dog in Michigan by the time I get through with you.
You want to do that?"

Buster took Willis's wrist in his mouth.

"Okay. We're going to do it. But I have to read the book first, so don't rush me."

They cut across backyards and followed alleys and dead-end streets, then the railroad track, and finally set off across a pine-studded pasture on a diagonal route toward home. It was slightly shorter than following the road, but it took longer to walk because of the hillocks of long grass, the small streams that had to be jumped or waded, the rocky outcroppings that had to be skirted. Still, it was a much more interesting walk than the roadside ditch, and there was no danger of Buster's being hit by a passing car.

Close to home they emerged from the trees into a square clearing that had, at one time, been a small private airstrip. The tiny hangar was now used for storing hay, and the landing strip was as much weed-filled cracks as it was blacktop.

At this point the pull of the book was stronger than the homing instinct. Willis veered toward his special place, his and Mary Lee's. It was a small grassy clearing behind the hangar, barely big enough to stretch out in. Young oak trees shaded the place from above, and a solid tangle of raspberry bushes crowded in from three sides. On one side, nearly hidden by the raspberries, was a head-high pile of old oil cans and bits of machinery. Three years ago he and Mary Lee had made a thorough search of the pile, looking for anything that seemed interesting. They hadn't found much, but the search had given Willis a proprietary feeling about the junk pile. He knew exactly what was in there, and if he ever wanted any of it, there it was.

Today he didn't even look at the junk pile. He took only enough time to pick and eat a double handful of raspberries. Then, after wiping his hands thoroughly on the grass, he opened the book.

The next day, Buster's formal training began. Every morning Willis took him to the airstrip, where they could be alone, without the noises and diversions of the sawmill. The book said to keep the lessons short, so they worked for fifteen or twenty minutes at a time, and rested or walked or roughhoused in between. By the end of the first morning Buster was sitting and heeling on command.

As the book suggested, Willis scolded only gently and praised mightily, and Buster relished the training. He was a dog of high intelligence, and he had an extremely close, loving relationship with his trainer. The rapport was strong between them. Training was almost ridiculously easy.

On the fourth day of the lessons Mary Lee begged to be included. "Peaches could learn, too. I'll train her while you train Buster. You can tell me what to do. Okay?"

Willis hesitated. He loved the training time, alone at the airstrip with Buster. But on the other hand, Peaches was such a stupid little dog that it would be worth having Mary Lee around, just to show off Buster's superiority.

"Okay, you can come, but you have to do exactly what I tell you."

When they got to the airstrip, Willis said, "Okay now, come out here where it's paved. This is the training ring, from here over to there and around. You can use the leash. Buster doesn't need it anymore." He handed her the clothesline-rope noose he had been using.

"Now look, you put it around her neck like this, see? So it pulls up and chokes her when she doesn't do right."

"Oh, I don't want to choke her!"

"It doesn't hurt them, stupid. All dogs get trained that way. As soon as she minds, you let up on the pressure. Now I'll yell 'heel,' and you have to make her walk right beside your left leg. She can't get ahead or drop behind, either one. And when you stop, tell her to sit, and make her sit down. Got it?"

"Yep."

They lined up, Willis and Buster in front, Mary Lee and Peaches behind.

"Okay, here we go," Willis said. "Buster, heel!"

Around the paved square they went, around and around. Buster paced himself so that his head was always beside Willis's left knee. His tail moved with suppressed pleasure. He was intent on Willis. When Willis stopped, Buster sat immediately, squarely, proudly.

Mary Lee's commands began in the same businesslike tone as Willis's, but after three rounds they had risen to tense, sharp sounds. The little white dog fought the rope. She pulled in all directions and tried to chew the rope. She sat down and had to be dragged. When Mary Lee commanded her to sit, she braced against the girl's pushing hand. At one point she whirled and snapped at Mary Lee's wrist as the girl tried to force her down into the sitting position.

"I just can't make her do anything," Mary Lee wailed. "She's just stupid!"

Willis had an uncommon feeling of compassion toward his sister. He imagined how he would feel if the dog he owned and loved were making such a miserable showing.

"Here, I'll take her around once," he said. "You hang onto Buster."

As Willis changed places with Mary Lee, Buster whined and lunged toward him. Mary Lee had to brace herself to keep the dog from getting away from her.

"You stay with Mary Lee for a minute. I'll be right back."

Willis took the rope and commanded Peaches to heel. The combination of the stronger hand and voice, and her weariness from the last struggle, had a quieting effect on Peaches. She still fought the rope but not as violently, and on the fourth try she allowed herself to be pushed down into a sit.

"Good girl! Good Peaches, that was wonderful." Because the book called for elaborate praise, Willis hid his secret gloating over the dog's stupidity, and dropped to his knees to hug her and congratulate her.

Suddenly there was a growl, a shout from Mary Lee, and Buster was between Willis and Peaches, attacking the little dog, snarling, thrashing his head from side to side. The dogs were a blur of motion. Peaches' voice came ki-yiing up from the bottom of the blur.

Mary Lee screamed.

Willis yelled at Buster, but the dog was beyond hearing him. The boy grabbed double handfuls of Buster's back, but the dog lunged out of his fingers.

It lasted less than a minute. Then, as suddenly as it had begun, it was ended. Peaches dove for the sanctuary of Mary Lee, and Buster came to stand in front of Willis. The dog's eyes had an out-of-focus look to them, and his teeth were chattering from the tension in his jaws. Willis squatted and took Buster in his arms. He held him close, and he trembled with the dog.

When the moment was past, Willis went to look at Peaches.

"He almost killed her," Mary Lee said. She was crying from the after-tension.

"Oh, he did not. Here, let me look. She's just got one little cut place on her face there."

"And her ear."

"Oh, yeah. Well, she got off pretty light. If he'd really wanted to kill her, she'd have been one dead dog by now."

Mary Lee sniffed. "What made him do it, Willis? They never fought before, in all this time."

Willis went back to his dog and gave him the "come up" signal. Buster rose to stand chest to chest against Willis, his head on the boy's shoulder. Quietly, more to Buster than to Mary Lee, he said, "No, but I never made a fuss over Peaches before, either."

He thought about how he felt sometimes when Red or Mrs. Crosley paid attention to Mary Lee and not to him. He understood perfectly why Buster had wanted to kill Peaches.

It wasn't until much later that he began to wonder what had made Buster stop the fight, to let Peaches up when he could easily have killed her.

CHAPTER NINE

A BELL SHRILLED.

"Okay, dismissed. Be sure your tools are all put away properly," the instructor chanted.

Willis enjoyed woodshop more than any of his other classes, not only because it was the last class of the day, but also because he had a certain prestige in this class. He had exaggerated somewhat when he told the others he had spent the summer running the big saw at the mill, but there was enough truth in his tone to command a shade of respect.

He had been in seventh grade for a month now, and he was surprised to find that at times he nearly enjoyed school. The time passed much faster, walking from class to class, than it had when he had been forced to sit in the same seat all day, every day. At first it had been frightening and confusing, keeping the schedule straight and adjusting to five teachers instead of one, but by now he had the hang of it.

Woodshop was actually fun. He was making a birdhouse. They hadn't let him make the doghouse he had his heart set on, because of the cost of the lumber, but at home he was making sketches of the doghouse he was going to build from scraps of ship-lap from the mill. It would be for Peaches, since Buster lived in the shack. Peaches had never gotten very housebroken, so she lived outside, and winter wasn't far away.

Reluctantly he put away his sandpaper and the squares of redwood that would eventually be a birdhouse. The rest of the class was gone by now. That was the way he liked it. When they left ahead of him, there was no danger of everyone else group-ing together for the walk back to the main building, leaving him out of their groups.

The shop was in a part of the long, low concrete structure that comprised the bleachers for the foot-ball field, on top, and the locker rooms, band rooms, and supply rooms, beneath. It was behind the twin brick blocks of the junior high and high school build-ings, beyond the parking lot.

Willis came out into the October afternoon and took a deep breath. The best part of the day was close at hand, the moment when the bus stopped at his road and Buster flung himself up into Willis's hug.

A bit of gravel from the parking lot was sud-denly inside his right shoe, gouging into the side of his foot. He sat down on a concrete window well to get it out. The window behind him was frosted so he couldn't see in, but he knew it was the locker room the football players used. Willis could hear, through the slightly opened window, the sounds of the Junior Varsity team changing into their practice clothes.

A voice shouted, "Cripes, I can't find my wallet. Have any of you guys—oh, never mind, here it is."

Willis's finger paused in its probing for the rock. All those pairs of trousers in that locker room, most with wallets in them—most of the wallets with at least a few dollars inside. And for the space of probably an hour or so every afternoon at this time, all the players and both of the coaches were out on the field.

He stood up and walked slowly toward his bus. It was a possibility, something to think about. A possible start at being a master thief.

But on the other hand, there was the newer possibility, the one that he had been playing with ever since summer, of maybe being a dog trainer instead. And just lately he had found himself thinking about being a carpenter, a master cabinetmaker. The woodshop instructor had told him he had ability.

Ability. Willis cherished the teacher's praise.

All the way home on the bus he thought about how a person would go about getting into that locker room unnoticed, about how much money there would probably be, about what he could buy with it—a regular training collar and leash for Buster, a good book on being a dog trainer. Maybe a new rifle.

He thought about getting caught. He was still on probation from last year. Getting caught stealing again could mean only one thing. The state training school for boys. Years of being separated from Buster.

Buster. He thought about the way the dog stood up against him and stared deep into his eyes, and felt his thoughts. Could a dog tell if you were a thief? Would a dog still love you if you were?

The idea of all that money began to sour.

The bus slowed for their stop, and Willis and Mary Lee came together at the front rail to wait for the door to hiss open. Buster sat in his usual place, but Peaches wasn't in sight.

"Wonder where Peachie is?" Mary Lee said as they jumped from the bus.

A car approached, ignored the bus's stop sign, and whooshed around, throwing gravel against the yellow flank of the bus. Suddenly the car slammed to a skidding halt.

An impact—a high yelp.

The small white form arced through the air and fell into the grass of the drainage ditch.

"Peaches," Mary Lee sobbed.

Willis stood frozen in place, both of his hands clutching Buster's ruff. The scene played itself out before his eyes, but he couldn't move. The woman in the car got out and stood looking down at Peaches, crying and repeating over and over that she hadn't even *seen* the dog and that she'd be glad to pay for a new one. All of the bus riders had gotten out and were standing about uncomfortably, saddened by the sight but not knowing what to do. Mary Lee was sobbing in the arms of the bus driver.

Finally the woman left and the bus driver motioned his charges back aboard. To Mary Lee he said, "Are you sure you don't need any help, sis?"

She shook her head. "My brother will help me."

Then they were gone, and it was just Mary Lee and Willis and Buster sniffing in a puzzled way at the still white mound.

"Come on," Willis said. "Let's go home. We'll bury her, and fix up a nice grave and everything."

He wrapped Peaches in his jacket so he wouldn't have to look at her, then picked her up and started down the road with Buster pacing beside him, subdued. Mary Lee walked behind.

All the way home one thought beat against the inside of Willis's head. It could have been Buster.

What if it had been Buster?

He began to feel the despair of losing his own dog. It was more than he could stand. A pair of tears spotted the jacket he carried. He wiped his nose on his shirt sleeve.

They buried Peaches at the airstrip, where it was unlikely that anyone would find the grave. Willis dug the hole while Mary Lee pulled goldenrod stalks and bittersweet berries. They lined the grave with long soft meadow grass and, when it was refilled, heaped the flowers on top.

"I'll make a marker in woodshop, with her name on it," Willis said.

Mary Lee nodded.

Suddenly Willis heard himself say, "Listen, you can have Buster if you want him."

Mary Lee's reddened eyes opened wide and stared at him. For a long time she didn't speak, and Willis was rigid with fear that she would say yes.

Finally she swallowed and whispered, "That's the first really good thing you ever did in your life. I'll remember it forever and ever."

Willis forced himself to say, "Well, do you want him or not?"

Again there was an agonizing pause. The stillness in the clearing echoed against Willis's ears.

Slowly Mary Lee shook her head from side to side. "Just because I lost my dog, that doesn't mean we both have to. Besides, you couldn't give Buster away even if you wanted to. He'd never love anybody else but you. And besides that, if I took him, you'd probably beat the living daylights out of me."

She looked down and allowed a small smile to twitch her mouth. Suddenly the tension around them broke. They stood up and turned toward home.

"You're damn right," he said, laughing. "But you can pet him whenever you want to."

In spite of the sadness of the day, Willis felt a sudden blooming of happiness.

CHAPTER TEN

H EY, WILLIE, you going to the game tonight?"

Willis just shook his head. The school bus was slowing for his stop, and Mary Lee was already at the front.

It was a stupid question, anyway, and it didn't deserve an answer, Willis thought angrily. Those guys knew very well he didn't have seventy-five cents to waste on tickets for a football game. And he didn't care anything about football anyway. That was for the big guys. Willis had already built a strong defensive dislike for school sports so that he could refuse them before they refused him.

But football faded from his mind the moment the bus door opened.

Buster wasn't there.

Mary Lee and Willis stared at each other, and shared the fear. Just two weeks ago it had been

Peaches who wasn't at the bus, and then she was dead.

Frantically they began to call Buster's name.

Hardly daring to do it, Willis looked along the ditches on both sides of the road, dreading to find a still brown heap. There was none. Mary Lee stood in the center of the mill road, rotating slowly, calling, searching for movement among the trees. There was none.

"Maybe he's home," she called. "Maybe he got his time mixed up or something."

They started home, but Willis refused to be cheered. He was positive that nothing short of death would keep Buster from meeting the bus. Halfway home, his steps quickened into a jog, and then a headlong run.

Buster was nowhere around the mill nor the shack.

Mary Lee said, "Let's go ask Mrs. Crosley," and Willis forgot his dislike for the big brown house and the woman who so clearly preferred Mary Lee to him. Together they ran across the road and up onto the Crosleys' front porch.

Mrs. Crosley opened the door before they could knock.

"Have you seen Buster?" Mary Lee panted. "He didn't meet the bus."

The woman frowned. "No, I haven't seen him all day. Where do you reckon he went?"

"We don't know," Willis said in a cracking voice. "But he wouldn't miss that bus unless he was

68

. . ." He couldn't say the word. His throat was swelling painfully. Never had he known such fear, never since the shadowed time when his mother was suddenly gone from his life. He felt detached from the floor, as though he could be tipped over and blown away.

He felt Mrs. Crosley's hand on his arm, holding him firm against his fear. "You kids come on in. We'll call the sheriff and see if anybody reported a dog hit by a car. Then you can get that off your minds."

Willis and Mary Lee stood in the middle of the purple and brown living room while Mrs. Crosley dialed the phone. Willis was unaware that he was clutching Mary Lee's hand.

"Hello, sheriff's office? This is Mrs. Carl Crosley, out to the sawmill. Listen, I was wondering, has anybody reported a dog hit by a car out our way? It was a big brown kind of collie type, or shepherd or some such. There's a couple of kids here that are sort of worried about him. Wasn't, huh?"

She smiled at Willis and shook her head. His arms and legs began to tremble.

She was listening again and smiling. "Over at Art Meyer's by Five Corners? Yes, that's not too far from here. Well, I expect that's what it was then. Thank you a lot. Sorry to bother."

She hung up. "You know where Five Corners is?" she asked, still smiling. Willis nodded. "Do you know that yellow house about half a mile this side of the Corners, with a roadside stand out in front?"

Mary Lee jumped up and down. "I know it.

We got a pumpkin there one time at Halloween. Is Buster there?" Her voice squeaked with excitement.

"Well, I don't know for sure, but the man in the sheriff's office said Art Meyer's retriever is in season, if you know what that means, and he said every time she's in season, every male dog for miles around is over there trying to get into her pen. So that's probably where Buster is."

A heaviness settled in Willis's stomach. Buster wouldn't be at Meyer's place. It would take a heck of a lot more than a female dog in season to keep Buster away from him. He knew it. He knew how much *he* hated the forced hours away from the dog. It had to be the same for Buster.

Mary Lee broke into his thoughts. She was dragging him out of the house and saying, "Hurry up, Willis. Let's go over there."

"No." He pulled loose from her and looked away from her puzzled face. "You go on home. I want to go by myself."

He left her staring after him, and loped up the road. There was still a chance Buster might be at the bus stop.

He wasn't.

There was a chance he might be anywhere along the road between there and Five Corners. Willis ran, then walked, then ran again when the pain left his side, and every quarter mile or so he stopped and called.

No dog appeared.

The afternoon shadows were long and dim by

the time the yellow house came into sight. The air was cooling into evening, but Willis was sweaty. He could make out a small fenced enclosure behind the garage. There was movement around the pen—several small shapes pacing, avoiding each other, walking the length of the pen, while the dog inside paced along with them.

Willis stared at the pacing dogs as his legs carried him closer. He prayed that Buster was there, alive, not hit by a car.

And he prayed that he wasn't.

Two of the dogs were big ones. One was light-colored. The other—the other was Buster.

Willis leaned against the back of the roadside stand. He had neither the breath nor the spirit to call out to his dog. This, then, was the reason Buster had failed to meet the bus. Not death, not mortal wounds, tragic but beyond the will of the dog. Just this.

This betrayal.

His voice trembled with rage when he called the dog's name.

Instantly Buster turned, wagged his tail, trotted to Willis. But he didn't jump up on the boy. He came close enough for Willis's fingers to brush his coat, but then he danced away and rejoined the other dogs.

Willis stared after him, but his eyes were blinded by the old red fury, the terrible shaking, mind-blocking fury that took over his body.

He did not hear his own voice saying, over and

over, "Okay for you. Okay for you." He was only distantly aware of walking along the highway, then riding in someone's car, and then walking again, in town now, at the school, across the parking lot filled with cars. The high white lights were on above the football field, and the bleachers were overflowing with dark, moving human shapes.

There were no conscious thoughts in Willis's head, only instinctive actions that followed preset patterns. Speaking to no one, he slipped down the broad cement stairs that led beneath the bleachers. Through the band room he went, through another small room. Then he was stopped by a locked door. With smooth unconscious movements he reversed, went back through the band room, up the stairs, out into the night, and along the front of the building to the window well where he had sat to take the stone out of his shoe.

I never loved you anyway. I don't need you.

The loose thoughts floated in the blankness of his mind, and he didn't even know they were there.

Without looking to see whether anyone was watching, he dropped down into the window well. The window was closed. He pushed up, but it didn't give. The window was fighting him, too, just like everything else in the world. He kicked the frosted glass, and it shattered.

A lovely, slow shattering of glass fragments.

He reached inside, undid the lock, and slid the window up. Blood dripped steadily from his arm and his ankle, but he didn't know it.

72

All those wallets were waiting for him, all that money. Dog trainer, hah! He was a master thief.

He wriggled through the window.

One other time, he remembered vaguely, he had climbed through a window. . . .

"All right, buddy, just what the hell do you think you're doing?" The voice came from one of the faces that stared at him. One of the coaches. The room was brightly lit and filled with boys who stood like startled birds, halfway through the act of changing their clothes.

Willis was confused. He was waking from a dream. He couldn't think where he was nor how he got there. And yet his mouth was smiling.

CHAPTER ELEVEN

DURING THE HOUR'S WAIT for the probation officer to drive down from Whitewater, Willis sat on a green metal typist's chair in the principal's office. The chair had no arms, and he felt in constant danger of toppling off.

He thought no thoughts at all; he just waited. It was done now, and whatever was going to happen to him was beyond his control. He had a peculiar feeling of having taken a necessary first step toward something inevitable and right.

The principal was there to watch him. He had been called from his house three doors down from the school, and he was openly annoyed at having to leave his television program. He and Willis sat in silence. Outside the office window, the stadium lights shone and the loudspeaker called the action of the football game.

Eventually Willis heard the hard quick steps of Mr. Hein in the hall, then in the outer office.

"Well, Willis," Mr. Hein said in a dry tone, standing close to Willis and looking down at him.

Mr. Hein was a very young man, still in college pimples and long hair. Behind his glasses his pale eyes were usually kind. They were not kind tonight.

The principal rose and moved toward the door. "Well, Mr. Hein, here's your troublemaker. You can take care of this now without me, can't you? You'll be sure and lock the door when you leave?"

Mr. Hein nodded and turned his attention to Willis.

"Okay, tell me what happened."

Willis hesitated. Vaguely he wondered if there was any lie he could tell that would sound the least bit believable. Probably not, he decided. And somehow lying seemed to be more effort than it was worth.

"I broke the window in the stadium. In the locker room."

"I know that already. What I want to know is why, Willis?"

Willis shrugged.

"You thought the locker room would be empty by then, right?"

Willis was silent.

"Were you going to play a little sticky-fingers with the team's wallets or something like that?"

Willis stared straight ahead.

"But why, Willis, that's what I'd like to know. Last time we talked it seemed as though things were going along just fine for you. Was there a problem at school?"

"No."

"Did you need money for something in particular, that I don't know about?"

Willis shook his head.

"Trouble at home?"

Willis tightened his face so no emotion could slip out. He blocked out the picture of Buster turning away from him, trotting away with those other dogs. Going away.

Mr. Hein sighed and pushed up his glasses to rub the corners of his eyes.

"Okay, talkative Sam. We're playing your game, you know. It'll be Monday at the soonest before we can get you into Juvenile Court, and you'll have to wait in the county jail. After your hearing—"

"You mean right now, tonight? I can't even go home first?" Suddenly Willis longed for home. He had to see Buster.

Mr. Hein shook his head. "I can't let you go home, Willis. You don't have proper supervision at home, and you know it. You'd take off like a bunny rabbit as soon as I was out of sight. After your hearing you will undoubtedly be moving on to the training school, since you were already on probation. How long you have to stay there depends on—"

"But I *have* to go home first. Please, Mr. Hein, I just have to go home first." Willis was unaware of the tears that stood in his eyes. He only knew he had to get to Buster.

Mr. Hein hesitated. "What's so important at home?"

"My dog . . ."

77

Mr. Hein just shook his head and held the office door open for Willis. "I'm sorry, but you should have thought of your dog *before* you broke that window. Your dog will just have to get along without you. Come on. We've got a long drive."

"Come in, dear." Mrs. Crosley held open her kitchen door while Mary Lee stepped inside. "I thought I'd better tell you right away, even though your dad's—ah—out tonight. I just had a call from the principal at the high school. Here, sit down at the table there. A glass of milk?"

Mary Lee nodded. She already was sure it had something to do with Willis. It seemed to take Mrs. Crosley a long time to pour the glass of milk and spread a fistful of Oreo cookies on a saucer.

"There you are, dear. Now then, I have a little bad news for you about Willis. They arrested him a little while ago. No," she soothed away Mary Lee's panic, "it's nothing too terrible. Nothing too surprising, though, for Willis, if I may say so. He tried to break into the gym, or something, at the football game. He'll have to go to court next week, and after that I'm sure they'll send him to the state training school. You remember how close he came to being sent there the last time he got in trouble? Well, I'm afraid this time he's really done it. Honestly, I don't know what gets into that boy. Guess he's just a born troublemaker."

In spite of her foreboding, Mary Lee was surprised at the news. Willis had seemed so much better, so much nicer, lately, so wrapped up in Buster that he seemed to have forgotten about doing really bad things. Gradually Mary Lee began to realize that Willis was gone. She might not see him for a long, long time. It would be just her at home now, and occasionally Daddy. Her eyes and nose stung with oncoming tears.

"Oh, there now, dear, don't you worry." Mrs. Crosley held out her arms, and Mary Lee went to cry against her. "You can stay over here if you like. Don't worry now. Nothing bad's going to happen to Willis, or to you either, I promise."

Mary Lee luxuriated in the shelter of Mrs. Crosley, but she knew she couldn't stay. She had to be home when her father came back from wherever he was, so she could tell him about Willis. Even more important, she had to be home to take care of Buster. Willis would kill her if she let anything happen to Buster while he was in jail.

It was late the next afternoon when Buster came home. He came happily, wearily, limping slightly on one foot. When Mary Lee opened the door and called him inside, the dog bounded in, looking left and right, his ears flapping as he turned his head.

"Willis isn't here, Buster." Mary Lee spoke sadly but clearly, wanting the dog to understand as soon as possible and get it over with.

Buster moved around the two rooms, forgetting to limp in his eagerness to find Willis. He nosed under piles of dirty clothes, whining softly every now and then.

"I told you he's not here."

Buster went to the door and scratched at it.

"No, you can't go out. He's not anywhere around here, and he won't be for a long time, so you might as well get used to it."

She tore up a heel of bread and added it to the handful of rabbit meat scraps she'd been saving for him.

"Here."

She set it down, but Buster just went on digging at the door.

Days went by. The bread and rabbit meat dried, untouched. Mary Lee replaced them with fresh food on Monday. Buster sat staring at the door.

By the end of the week Buster was starting to get weak. He had drunk several times from the water bucket, but he refused to eat. When Mary Lee tried to push the food between his teeth, he turned his head away. Mary Lee continued to lock him in the shack when she left for school in the mornings, even though the dog no longer tried to get out. He seemed to be waiting, simply waiting. Big Red came and went as usual, stepping over the dog when he had to.

On Friday night Mary Lee opened her spiral-bound notebook and wrote Willis a letter. "Dear Willis, I am worried about Buster. . . ."

CHAPTER TWELVE

DEAR WILLIS,

I am worried about Buster. He hasn't eaten anything since you left. I think he is going to die. Please try to come home for a visit as soon as you can, so Buster won't die.

Your sister,
Mary Lee

P.S. We miss you. How are things there?

The fear that rippled through Willis as he read was like no other fear he had known. Buster was his only hold on the world, his only connection with anything solid. If Buster died . . .

He sat in the center of his cot, slowly picking away the ragged fringe of Mary Lee's notebook paper, along the edge where it had been torn from its spiral. On either side of his cot stretched nineteen more cots just like his. The room was large and bright and covered most of the third floor of Cottage A. The second floor was just like this one, a big room full of cots; the first floor was the lounge, kitchen, and huge dining room.

It was Tuesday afternoon. After a week at the training school Willis was beginning to feel somewhat settled in. The bigness of the place frightened him less, now. He still hated sleeping in a room with nineteen other boys plus a guard, only they didn't call them guards, who sat behind a raised desk all night and watched the sleepers. A monitor, they called him. Willis was even getting used to being watched by a monitor while he slept. The days were filled with meals, school, and talk sessions with the psychologist. It was not at all the terrible experience Willis had been braced for, but there were still the bars on the cottage windows, the knowledge that this was a jail, no matter how pleasant a jail.

And now Buster needed him and he was held here in this jail.

"Don't you worry, Buster," he said silently. "They can't keep me away from you."

He hadn't been there long enough to know whom to ask for permission to go home, but he decided to start with Mrs. Hill. She and her husband were the cottage parents for Cottage A, and she seemed to be a bit softer than her husband toward the boys. Willis found her in the kitchen, talking to a uniformed housekeeper.

"Mrs. Hill?"

"Just a minute, Willis, and I'll be right with you. Check with the laundry again, Mary; they've got to be there. Now then, what's the. trouble?" She turned her attention to Willis. She was young, plump, and pleasantly uncombed.

Willis handed her the letter.

"Buster's my dog," he said as she scanned the letter.

"I see. Well, I wouldn't worry about him if I were you. Dogs don't ever really starve to death, just because their owners go away."

"Yes, they do. Buster would. He really loves me, Mrs. Hill. I know he'd starve to death for me. Couldn't I go home and see him just for a day? If I could just talk to him and get him started eating, I know he'd be okay. I have to explain . . ."

Mrs. Hill looked down at him expectantly, but he couldn't finish the sentence. She wouldn't understand that Willis could talk to Buster. She wouldn't believe him. He could read it in her eyes, which looked down at him kindly but were gently making fun of his childishness.

"No, you couldn't possibly have a home visit this soon, Willis. Two months would be the very soonest you could be allowed a home visit, unless it was a family emergency."

"Well, what the hell do you think this is?" he shouted. "My dog is dying. If that's not an emergency, what is?" He wanted to punch her and punch her and punch her. But he held onto himself. This was too important for a rage.

"Is there somebody else I could ask? I just have to go home, Mrs. Hill."

She looked offended, then mildly relieved. "The superintendent would be the one, but he's attending a seminar in Detroit this week."

Willis felt the rage building up again. Tightly he said, "Who, then?"

"The assistant superintendent, I suppose. Mr. Blackman. You could talk to him, but I'm sure he'll tell you the same thing I did."

"Where is he?"

"Probably home by now. Do you know where he lives? It's the little green house just this side of the cattle barns. I'll give you a pass, but you must just go to Mr. Blackman's house and right straight back here, understand?"

Willis snatched the slip of paper from her and ran outside. At the sidewalk he veered right and continued to run, past the other cottages, past the school building and the administration building, past the auto shop and other buildings with uses still unknown to Willis. At the far end of the road were the barns and machine sheds, and the small green house that held Buster's life or death.

Mr. Blackman was in the front yard with his head under the raised hood of his car. He emerged and looked down at Willis while Willis fought for enough breath to speak.

"Sir, I have to go home, right away. I just got this letter." He held out Mary Lee's letter and waited with straining impatience while Mr. Blackman wiped the grease from his hands. Mr. Blackman was large, dark, heavy, with something of a panda look about him.

"Let's see, your name is—"

"Willis, sir. I just came last week."

"Yes. That's what I thought." The man scanned the letter and handed it back. "I'm sorry your dog is missing you, Willis, but he's not going to starve to death—you can take my word for that."

"But please. If I could just go home, just for one day. You see, I didn't get to see Buster before I came up here, and the last time I did see him I was kind of mad at him, so I *have* to get home to him, to tell him I'm not mad at him anymore. Then he'll start eating again. Please, Mr. Blackman. Mr. Hein told me I could go home for a visit sometimes."

"Well, yes, but not this soon. We have a very definite rule about that. No boy goes home for at least two months, generally longer. You see, you need time to make the adjustment here, before you can visit home. Home visits are often disturbing to a boy, emotionally, while he's making the adjustment, and—"

"I can't go."

"No. I'm sorry. Check with me again when you've been here two months, and we'll see what we can do then, all right?"

All the way back to the cottage, all through supper and the long evening, Willis fought to keep his head clear of the red rage. Buster needed him. He had to be able to think straight. He had to get out.

CHAPTER THIRTEEN

WILLIS LAY ON HIS COT, waiting for it to get late enough to start doing something. All the boys were in bed, but they were still tossing, coughing, whispering. The monitor sat at his raised desk reading a novel and glancing up every now and then to see if anyone needed settling down. Tonight's monitor was Mr. Hill. The cottage parents took turns at the night duty.

All evening Willis had been working at the problem of getting away. Once out of the cottage there would be no problem. The training school was huge, rambling, unfenced, and not far from a highway. He had his jeans on under his pajama bottoms, and the pajama tops looked enough like a shirt that clothes should not be a giveaway, once he got clear of the school and started hitching rides.

The problem was getting out of the cottage. Willis knew the doors were all solidly locked and wired to an alarm system. A window would be the only way, and all the windows in the dormitory room were barred and in full view of Mr. Hill. That left only the hall, the bathroom and closet at the end of the hall, and whatever might be downstairs in the way of unbarred windows.

Willis waited as long as he could, then got up and moved softly to Mr. Hill's desk.

"Bathroom, please?"

Mr. Hill looked up from his book and nodded.

Willis padded out into the hall and stood for an instant, thinking. There was the stairwell leading downstairs, and the bathroom door beyond it, and, across from the bathroom, the door to the supply closet. Silently he moved to the stairs and down to the first landing.

Someone was coming.

With pounding heart he ran back upstairs and into the bathroom. Safety. This was where he was supposed to be. But there wasn't much time before Mr. Hill would begin to wonder.

Windows.

There were three, along the back of the room, and they had no bars. But they were small and high, very high. Willis went to the end of the long bathroom and stood looking up at them. Two of the windows were too high for him to reach. The third was at the same height, but it was over a sink. Moving quickly but awkwardly, Willis climbed up onto the sink. He had no idea how much weight a sink could hold. The porcelain was slick, cold, achingly hard against his knees.

By steadying himself against the mirrored wall he managed to stand. He twisted and reached for the window. It opened at the bottom and swung outward, opening a square of freedom, one foot high and two feet wide.

Big enough.

Carefully Willis moved his feet until he could look out the window. It was a sheer drop to the paved parking area below. The cottage was built on a slope so that, although it was three stories high in front, it was four in the rear. Four stories down, and pavement.

A chill of wonderful fear held Willis. This was all the dangerous things he had ever wanted to do, all in one. Suddenly he knew that if there was any possible way he could lower himself out of this window, he was going to do it. If he fell, it might kill him. It would probably kill him. That knowledge was the ultimate excitement.

But how to do it?

He jumped down and made a swift search of the bathroom, aware now that he had been gone long enough from his bed. The bathroom held nothing that could possibly serve as a rope to lower himself down the wall.

He went out into the hall and across to the supply closet. It held only cleaning supplies—shelves of cleanser, rolls of toilet paper and paper towels, a broom, a drum of sweeping compound, a mop.

Desperately Willis stared into the closet. There had to be something, rags, towels, something he could tie together to make a rope.

Suddenly his gaze fixed on the mop. It was a large old-fashioned mop made of long strands of ropelike cord. Willis stared at the cord. It looked strong, not strong enough to hold him as it was, but maybe a braid of the cords, several strands thick, would hold. Surely it would.

The mophead was held together by a long metal clamp. Willis worked his fingertips under the clamp and pulled, hard. It sprang open.

The cords had only to be slipped off of the metal core and pulled loose from flimsy stitches that held them together.

Willis closed the closet door and ran back down the hall. Mr. Hill was just rising from his desk.

"Sorry I took so long," Willis whispered. "I think it was that cherry pie we had for supper."

Mr. Hill smiled. "Okay, g'night now."

Back in bed, Willis began his frantic arithmetic. Four stories. Probably ten feet high, each of them, including this one, since the window was so high up. Minus six feet or so that he could drop without getting hurt. Minus another six feet or so, the length of his body and arms, hanging from the end of the rope. So the rope would have to be at least twenty-eight feet long, plus a little for tying it to—to what?

The closest thing to the window that he could think of for anchoring the rope was the drainpipe under the sink. That would add another, say, six feet.

Okay. That'd make a total of thirty-four feet. The mop strings looked about two feet long, so that would mean he'd need at least seventeen braids, tied together.

There wouldn't be time.

Maybe they don't need to be braided, he thought. They'd be just as strong if I just tied them together. It shouldn't take too long to make the rope that way.

After what seemed a reasonable length of time he got up again. Mr. Hill just nodded to him as Willis walked out.

He ran to the closet and slipped the mophead off of the handle. Then he darted back into the bathroom and into one of the cubicles. If anyone came checking on him, he thought, he could just stuff the mop strings into the toilet tank.

With shaking fingers he began yanking the strings apart. The stitching was tougher than he'd thought. He jerked and jerked until the strings lay in a loose mound in front of him.

Now, how many? he thought, fighting down his tension. How many strings will make it strong enough?

He counted out six strands. Together they looked as thick as ropes he had swung from before. Thicker. He knotted the six together at the top, then pulled six more and tied them to the first strands. Then six more.

No more time, he told himself. I can't let Mr. Hill get suspicious.

As quietly as he could, he lifted the top off of the toilet tank and stuffed his short rope and the loose strings down inside.

An excited chant rang in his head: It's going to work; it's going to work.

He waited two hours, then made another trip. This time, working as fast as his fingers would go, he knotted length after length of the dripping strings. He pressed his luck and worked till all the strings were rope, braced to dump it into the tank if the bathroom door should open.

It was finished. Twenty lengths. Plenty long enough. Willis breathed faster, looking down at the pile of rope.

But he had been gone long enough. He put the rope into the tank and went back to bed. His body was strung with jumping nerves. He wanted to get on with it. Get it over with. His mind ran ahead, planning where to go when he got to the ground, which way to reach the highway without going near lighted areas or dogs.

When the clock above Mr. Hill said three o'clock, he got up again.

This was it.

He put on shoes and socks and hoped Mr. Hill wouldn't notice.

"Bathroom again, please," he whispered.

Mr. Hill's head jerked from his near-doze.

"Again? Are you sick?"

"Just got the trots."

"Maybe I'd better get you some medicine."

"No. Please. I'm in a hurry, sir. I don't need any medicine. I just need the bathroom."

"Well, okay, go ahead."

Sweat stood out on Willis's face as he ran from

the room, down the hall, into the intense familiarity of the third cubicle. He fished out the dripping rope and ran to the sink. All he needed now was for nobody to come in for the next few minutes. Then it would be all over. He'd be away, down the highway, heading for Buster.

He tied the rope hard and tight to the drainpipe, and climbed up onto the sink. His movements grew sure and smooth. He was going, maybe to freedom, maybe to death. He didn't know which. At that moment it didn't matter. There was no fear in him, only the deep shaking excitement of coming close to death.

The rope fell out and down, swaying, lashing gracefully in the blackness. With a jump, a kick, a twist, Willis squirmed through the window. The rope was in his hands. His knees and heels came through the window. His body twisted. The bricks scraped against his cheek, against his bare belly where his pajama top rode up. Hands on the rope, feet against the wall, he started down.

Above him a knot began to slip.

Willis screamed.

In the shack at Crosleys' Sawmill, the large brown dog came suddenly to his feet. He had not stood for two days, but there was no weakness in his stance. He sent a volley of barking through the shack, barking that changed to a wolf howl at the end.

93

Mary Lee jerked up from the sofa.

"Buster, what're you barking at? Why, you're standing up! What . . ."

The dog was staring at a spot near the door.

"There's nothing there, Buster."

There *was* nothing there, nothing her eyes could see. And yet Buster's tail began to move faster and faster. In his throat came the low keening sound he made when he greeted Willis at the school bus. The dog's eyes were alight with joy.

ALSO BY LYNN HALL

Fiction

Gently Touch the Milkweed
A Horse Called Dragon
Lynn Hall's Dog Stories
Ride a Wild Dream
Riff, Remember
The Secret of Stonehouse
The Shy Ones
The Siege of Silent Henry
Sticks and Stones
Stray
To Catch a Tartar
Too Near the Sun

Nonfiction

Kids and Dog Shows

ABOUT THE AUTHOR

The two main loves in Lynn Hall's life are writing and dogs. For several years she has devoted herself full-time to writing books for young readers, most of them fictional stories about dogs. *Troublemaker* is her fourteenth book for Follett.

Ms. Hall was born in a suburb of Chicago and was raised in Des Moines, Iowa. She has always loved dogs and horses and has kept them around her whenever possible. As a child, she was limited to stray dogs, neighbors' horses, and the animals found in library books. But as an adult, she has owned and shown several horses and has worked widely with dogs, both as a veterinarian's assistant and a handler on the dog show circuit. In recent years she has realized her lifelong dream of owning her own kennel and raising her own line of champion dogs; at her Touchwood Kennel she raises Bedlington terriers, which she shows throughout the country.

Ms. Hall lives in the village of Masonville, Iowa. Her leisure time is spent reading, playing the piano, or exploring the nearby hills and woodlands on horseback or foot, usually with a dog or two at her heels.